WHO STOLE The Wizard of Oz ?

by Avi
illustrated by
Derek James

Alfred A. Knopf 🐕 New York

Library of Congress Cataloging in Publication Data
Avi, 1937–   Who stole the Wizard of Oz? (Capers)
Summary: Becky and her brother use some ingenious clues
to identify the person who stole
five children's books from the town's library.
[1. Mystery and detective stories]   I. Title.   II. Series
PZ7.A953Wh   1981   [Fic]   81–884
ISBN 0-394-84644-3 (pbk.)   AACR2
ISBN 0-394-94644-8 (lib. bdg.)

For M. Jerry Weiss

CONTENTS

*WHO
STOLE
The
Wizard
of Oz
?*

1 ··· The Crime

My sister Becky and I were stretched out on the front porch one morning thinking out loud about how we should spend our summer vacation. It was too hot to do much more. At about nine-thirty, a police car turned down our street, then stopped in front of the Checkertown Library. Checkertown, Ohio—that's our town. Anyway, we watched the policeman go into the library, then we went back to making plans. But half an hour later, the phone rang. Becky jumped up, ran inside, and grabbed it. "Hello?"

"Is this Becky?"

"Yes."

"This is Mrs. Brattle. The Checkertown librarian."

"Oh, hi."

"Becky, there's a policeman here who wants to talk to you. Can you come over now?"

"What for?"

"There's been a robbery at the library, Becky," said Mrs. Brattle.

"What's that got to do with me?"

For a moment, Mrs. Brattle didn't say anything. "Please," she finally said, "just come. And I think you'd best bring one of your parents."

"They're not home. Neither is my Grandpa. Only my brother Toby is here with me.

Do you really think *I* took something?"

"You'd better bring Toby," said Mrs. Brattle, avoiding the question.

"What was stolen?"

"*The Wizard of Oz*," Mrs. Brattle said.

We headed toward the library slowly, so Becky could do some explaining. "There we were," she said. "It was yesterday, one hour before school let out. One hour before vacation. We were going crazy, Toby. Nobody could sit still. Not even Mr. Dawley. Then in walked Miss McPhearson."

"What's this have to do with Mrs. Brattle, the library, or *The Wizard of Oz?*" I asked.

"Just listen," she said. "I'm trying to tell you. When Miss McPhearson walked in, everything changed. It was like holding a balloon that pops."

I could understand that. Miss McPhearson—the sixth grade teacher and Becky's teacher next September—is tall, redheaded, straight, and stiff as wood. She looks like a queen—not a happy queen, but a queen all the same.

"Even Mr. Dawley took off the silly hat we'd given him," continued Becky. "She took the class right over and handed out her summer reading list. Boy, are you lucky you don't have *her* next year!"

"No mysteries, no make-believe, no romantic adventures," said Becky, imitating Miss McPhearson by standing on her toes, tilting up her chin, and looking down at me. "Children your age are beyond such nonsense. This list contains nothing but basic, *useful* information. Yuk!"

Wrinkling her nose, Becky added, "She said we had to write two book reports—two *well-written* book reports, please—with close attention to spelling and grammar. And she wants them on the first day of the new term."

Becky was really annoyed. I couldn't blame her.

I might as well explain that Becky and I

are twins. Other people make a big thing of it, but we don't. We're not at all alike. I keep cool. She always thinks big things are going to happen. Not me. She says whatever is on her mind, while I think a little more before I talk. Maybe it's being so different that makes us such good friends.

"Anyway," continued Becky, "I decided to get the reports over with. As soon as school was out, I went over to the library to get the books. Then I had this idea of getting a book for you."

"How come?"

"Just to be nice," Becky admitted. "You like magic stuff, right? So I looked for a copy of *The Wizard of Oz*. But Mrs. Brattle said someone had already taken it. Just as I was leaving, though, she called me back and pointed to a stack of books on the table."

" 'I've got a whole lot of children's books for the book sale tomorrow,' she said, holding up a copy of *The Wizard of Oz*. 'Come early and you can buy it. The

8

children's books will only be five cents apiece.' "

"I tried to buy it right then," Becky said, "but she wouldn't let me."

" 'Tomorrow, eleven sharp—first come, first served,' she insisted."

" 'Thanks, but no thanks,' I said. 'Tomorrow's vacation.' Then I came home."

By the time Becky had finished, we were at the library.

"That's the whole story?" I asked her. I thought it would be something more than that.

"That's it," insisted Becky. "And now she's hinting that *I* stole *The Wizard of Oz*."

"Did you?"

"Don't be stupid!"

"Well," I said, "let's tell them."

2 ··· *The Accusation*

The Checkertown library was made to look like an ancient Greek temple. It has long columns that support the front roof, steps running up between them, and wide wooden doors. That morning, there was a sign by the door:

Book Sale: Library Book Fund
Saturday 11:00 a.m. to 3:00 p.m.

Becky tried the front doors, but they were locked. She was so upset that she began to shake them as if everything was the door's fault.

"Come on, Becky," I said, "let's do this right." And I knocked.

Mrs. Brattle, the librarian, opened the door and poked her head out.

"Oh, Toby," she said. "I'm glad you came too."

Mrs. Brattle reminds me of a sparrow. She's very small, and she always wears brownish clothes that are usually slightly wrinkled. Jumpy and nervous, she runs everywhere, keeping the whole library going by herself.

"Now this wasn't my idea," said Mrs. Brattle as she let us in. "The policeman is very impatient and can hardly be bothered. *He* wanted to see you. That is, after I told him about—I think I had best let him explain," she said, as we followed her into the main reading room.

The reading room is large, with a round, high-domed ceiling that always keeps everything quiet and cool. Bookcases stick out like spokes from round walls. Right in the center are three tables, some chairs, a globe, and a newspaper and magazine rack. Mrs. Brattle's desk is at the back, facing the entrance. Behind the desk is the reference shelf.

Off in one wing of the building, down a little hallway, is the children's room. There's a tall mirror in that hallway. It lets whoever sits at the desk keep an eye on what's going on in that room.

Mrs. Brattle's office looked like a bird's nest: books, papers, catalog cards all over. But seated behind the desk was this sharp-looking policeman writing on a pad.

Mrs. Brattle was uneasy. "This is the girl I mentioned," she said, "but I truly don't think—"

The policeman cut her off. "Better let me handle this," he said. From the look on his face, I could tell right off that he found the whole thing a joke.

"Becky," he began, "I understand you were in the library yesterday afternoon."

"Yes," said Becky.

"She comes all the time," put in Mrs. Brattle. "One of our best readers. Very polite. Always—"

12

"Mrs. Brattle," said the policeman, "you *did* request help." He turned back to Becky. "You asked for a particular book, Becky. Remember which?"

"Sure. *The Wizard of Oz.* I was getting it for Toby."

"Now, Becky," said the policeman, "Mrs. Brattle showed you a copy of that book, which was to be placed on sale. She said you

13

could have it if you came back this morning. You said you couldn't wait."

"I didn't say *that*," objected Becky.

After a quick glance at Mrs. Brattle, the policeman continued, "This morning when Mrs. Brattle arrived that book was gone. From what I can determine, someone came in the back door and took *The Wizard of Oz*. Was it you?"

Becky shook her head hard. "Not me!"

The policeman smiled. "Now, I'm going to read the names of some other books: *Winnie-the-Pooh*, *The Wind in the Willows*, *Through the Looking Glass and What Alice Found There*, *Treasure Island*. Ever hear of them?"

"Sure," said Becky.

The policeman looked smug. "When Mrs. Brattle checked this morning, those books were also missing."

"They're just kids' books, you know," said Becky.

"How much did you say those books were worth?" the policeman asked Mrs. Brattle.

The librarian became even more nervous. "Well, I'm really not sure. A lot perhaps. Maybe three thousand dollars."

"I don't believe it," Becky said right away.

The policeman seemed to be having trouble believing it himself. "Mrs. Brattle says they were rare books."

"I only said they *might* be," Mrs. Brattle quickly put in.

"Then what were they doing in the book sale?" I asked.

"Who is this boy?" the policeman wanted to know.

"My brother," said Becky. "And he's right. If the books were so valuable, how come they were being sold for a nickel?"

In a small voice, Mrs. Brattle said, "It was a mistake."

"Whatever it was, Becky," said the policeman, "Mrs. Brattle thinks you may be involved. Now look," he said, "if you took them, wouldn't it save a lot of fuss just to give them back?"

15

"I didn't take them," insisted Becky. She was getting angry.

The policeman looked from Mrs. Brattle to Becky. Then he lifted his hands and slapped them on his knees. "What do you want me to do, Mrs. Brattle? The boy's right. If they were valuable, they shouldn't have been going for a nickel. I don't think we can spend much time looking for twenty-five cents worth of books," he concluded. He stood up.

Mrs. Brattle seemed to be having a lot of trouble deciding what to do. She sat down and slumped in her seat.

"I'll put in my report," said the policeman. "Give me a call when you decide." Then he left.

"Do you really think I took them?" demanded Becky. I could see she really felt insulted.

"I don't know what to think," said Mrs. Brattle, pressing a nervous hand over her eyes. Then, glancing at her watch, she sud-

16

denly stood up. "Forgive me," she said. "I must get ready. The book sale is at eleven."

There was nothing for us to do but go home.

3 ... *First Clues*

When we got home, Becky and I headed for the porch where we could get out of the heat and talk about what had happened.

"It's wild," Becky said after a time. "Kids' books being worth so much. She made them sound like treasure—real treasure."

"You think it's true?"

"She wouldn't make such a fuss if it wasn't."

"You know," Becky said after a while, "if we found out who really took those books, she couldn't blame me."

"I know," I agreed. "It would be nice if we could."

"I think we'd better," said Becky. "I hate

people thinking I would steal something."

"We don't have much to go on," I warned her.

"Sure we do," she insisted. "We know the names of the stolen books. They were in the library. I mean, they were there yesterday. And this morning they were gone."

"And we know that they were worth a lot of money," I added.

"Mrs. Brattle only said *maybe*," Becky pointed out. "Toby," she said, climbing into the porch rocker, "those books had to come from someplace. People give old books to the library all the time. I bet if we found out who gave those, it would be a start."

"No point asking Mrs. Brattle. She's not going to say," I told her. As I watched the heat simmer off the top porch rail, I had a new thought. "When someone gives *you* a book, what do you do with it?" I asked.

"Read it."

"No, before that."

"What are you thinking?" Becky asked.

"You put your *name* in it."

"So what?" she asked, not getting my point.

Hoping I was making sense, I began, "Mrs. Brattle said that all those books were part of the book sale, right?" Becky nodded. "Maybe those five books were part of a whole bunch of books that *one* person gave. Then, *maybe* they had names in them. If we look in the books that are still at the sale, we might find a name—or something. It's a start."

Becky jumped up. "Fantastic!" she yelled. "Let's go!"

In one-half of a second, we were racing down the street. Just minutes after eleven, we reached the library basement where the sale was taking place. It was wild: people grabbing books, people trying to hold on to as many books as possible, people pushing ahead of other people. You would have thought gold was being given away!

A big, bald man with a goatee was in

charge. Becky whispered that he was Mr. Neal—and told me to watch out because he didn't like kids. He was sitting behind a little desk with a money box in front of him. Next to the box was a sign:

BOOKS 50¢
PAPERBACKS 15¢
CHILDREN'S BOOKS 5¢

"Open all the kids' books and see if there are any names in them," I said, starting at one end of the table marked 'Children.' Becky worked the other end.

At his desk, Mr. Neal kept a sharp eye on us. But we kept on opening and closing books, picking them up, and putting them down.

"Any luck?" Becky asked.

"Some. What about you?"

21

"I think so," she called. I could see she was excited.

All of a sudden, Mr. Neal got up and strode over. "What are you kids doing?" he demanded.

"Just looking," I managed to say.

"Looking or buying?" he wanted to know.

Becky came to the rescue. "Buying," she announced, showing him a nickel in the palm of her hand.

"Anyway," Mr. Neal grumbled, "be careful. They're old." Then he made his way back to guard the money box.

It took us about twenty minutes to go through all the books.

"Let's get out of here," I said.

"We've got to buy something," Becky reminded me.

Seeing a book that looked interesting—*Curious Facts About Ohio*—I took that.

As soon as we paid Mr. Neal his nickel, we ran outside. But we didn't go five steps before stopping. "You first," I said.

22

"Three names," she recalled. "David Block. There were three with his name. Ann Parker. Six from her. But most of them came from someone called Gertrude Tobias. There were at least twenty with her name."

"I found a couple from that Ann Parker too," I said. "But almost all the rest were from that one you found—Tobias. Who's she?"

"Maybe Gramp will know!"

And Becky tore down the street while I hurried to catch up.

4 ··· *Plan into Action*

Grandpa lives with us. He's a plumber, and he does jobs all over town. I don't think there's a house in Checkertown that he hasn't worked on. So, he knows everybody. And one of the best things about Gramp is that you can ask him anything, and he'll give you an answer—but he won't try to find out why you're asking.

We tracked him down to where he was working—in a ditch with lots of mud.

"Broken pipe," he told us. "Want to come in? The muck's fine."

"We want to ask you about some people," said Becky.

"Shoot," said Gramp. I think he was glad to rest a while.

24

I listed the names we found.

"Know 'em all," he said. Becky actually clapped her hands.

"David Block had a water problem in his basement," he said. "Got sick and moved out East six years ago."

"He's out," I said to Becky.

"Ann Parker," continued Grandpa.

"I have an idea," I said after a while. "Read the books—you know, the ones on her summer reading list. Then make your reports and take them to her. She'll think you're great. Bet she'd talk then."

Becky considered this. "I'd have to read the books," she said. "And that would take the rest of the day. What are you going to do?" she asked me. "Go out and play?"

"First I'll find where Miss McPhearson lives. Then I'll read too," I said, thinking it would help. "Look," I told her, "what would you rather do, have people think you stole those books or find who really took them?"

The rest of Saturday we spent on the porch reading. It was so hot, that was the best thing to do anyway. Becky had picked a book on bees and one about the life of Helen Keller. She wasn't bored at all.

Finding Miss McPhearson's address was easy. It was listed in our school guide. Then I checked it against the Checkertown map in the phone book. That done, I started reading *Curious Facts About Ohio*. Every once in a while I'd call out things like, "Did you know Ohio used to be part of Massachusetts?"

By dinner time Becky had finished reading her two books. Then she began writing, while I went on with that *Ohio* book. By nine o'clock she had finished both reports.

"Know why Checkertown is called Checkertown?" I asked her.

"No, and I don't want to," she said.

"You should," I told her. "It's our town, we live in Ohio, and it's in this book. Checkertown," I read, "A small town in Eastern Ohio named that because of the annual checker contest held in the old Railway Hotel. The railroad section manager, who planned the town and laid out its streets, was so taken with the game of checkers that he designed the town streets in checkerboard fashion: eight streets running one way and eight the other. There's even a map of the town," I told Becky. I showed it to her—or at least I tried to.

29

"Here she comes," I announced.

Miss McPhearson came out, shutting the door quickly behind as if she didn't want anyone to go in. In a shirt and slacks, she looked younger and nicer than at school. Her red hair wasn't tied up either and was pretty to look at. She didn't look like a mad queen to me. In fact, she didn't look mad at all, just puzzled.

"Are you looking for me?" she asked.

"Miss McPhearson," said Becky, speaking nervously, "I'm Becky Almano. I'm in your class next year, and you gave us some reading to do. I did two book reports, and here they are." Becky held out the papers.

Miss McPhearson seemed confused at first. But when she looked the papers over, she understood and smiled. "That's very good of you," she said, handing them back. "You must be a hard worker. I'll enjoy having you in my class. If you'd like some extra credit, why don't you read some more?" Then she started to go back in.

Becky was caught not knowing what to say.

When I saw what was happening, I quickly asked, "Miss McPhearson, was Gertrude Tobias your aunt?"

She turned around to look at me. "Yes," she said. Her voice dropped to a whisper. "Why do you ask?"

6 ... *Trying to Understand*

When we got home, we found the newspaper on the front walk. The paper is pub-
lished in Allerton, a nearby city. But it has a
special Checkertown section written by a
friend of Mom's. We always read it.

That day there were *two* stories in the
section, both under one headline: "Robber-
ies." One was about a break-in at a local gun
shop. The other one—the one that interest-
ed us—was about the library. Becky read it
out loud: *"Mrs. R. B. Brattle, Checkertown
librarian, reported a curious theft of books from
the Free Library sometime between Friday night
and Saturday morning. The books had been laid
out for the annual sale. An unidentified young*

person was questioned by the police, but according to Mrs. Brattle, the case was not pursued for lack of evidence. Total receipts at the book sale, which took place as scheduled, came to eighty-four dollars and twenty-five cents. Mrs. Brattle said it would be a great help to this year's book budget."

"Toby," said Becky when she'd finished. "If people find out that I'm that 'young person,' I'll die."

I shook my head. "I don't think Mrs. Brattle is going to tell," I told her. "I mean, there's nothing here about how the books were worth anything either. That was her mistake. She said so. I think she wants to forget the whole thing."

"But what if someone saw me go into the library yesterday morning," Becky went on.

"Becky, no one cares!" I yelled at her.

"I do!" she yelled back. "Don't you see, unless we find out who took those books, people will still think it's me."

So there it was. We still had to find out the truth. Miss McPhearson hadn't told us

reaching for her phone. "Whom shall I say is calling?"

"She doesn't know us," I had to admit.

The woman frowned. "What do you want to see her about? She doesn't have money to spend on cookies or things like that."

"We want to ask her about a Miss Tobias. It's important."

The woman picked up the phone and dialed. It took a while before anyone answered. "Mrs. Chesterton? This is the desk. I hope I didn't wake you—good. There are two youngsters here to see you—that's right, children. They want to talk to you about Miss Tobias—"

She put the phone down. "Miss Chesterton says to come up. Second floor. Room two-fifteen. Take those steps. And don't stay long," the woman called as we started up. "She works nights, and I do think we woke her."

When we found room 215, we knocked carefully.

"Come in," called a soft voice.

Inside we found a small bright room with large windows overlooking the street. A four-poster bed, dresser, chair, and a small table (with an electric hot plate on it) were the only pieces of furniture. Everything was covered with white lace, like clouds.

Seated by the window was a small lady. Her arms were thin and so were her ankles. She had white hair, pale skin, and fine lacy lines all over her face. She almost seemed to be made of lace too. She was wearing a gray robe.

"Are you Mrs. Chesterton?" we asked, standing by the door. It felt odd to be there.

"Yes I am," the woman answered in a small voice. Her eyes were dark but bright against that small face. She reminded me of a kitten.

"Can we speak with you?" Becky said carefully.

Mrs. Chesterton smiled. "Of course. It's nice to have visitors. Just shut the door so we

7 ··· The Tale of Miss Tobias

"Once upon a time Miss Tobias was rich and thought herself most clever," began Mrs. Chesterton, as if telling a fairy tale. "She was not always a nice person, but she did love children. I will say that. Why, sometimes she used to go to the library here in town and sit with them in the children's room reading stories. That's how much she enjoyed their company. They liked her, too, and would even tell her their secrets.

"Now, Miss Tobias could have married if she'd wanted to. Many times. But you see, she was full of smart ideas. When she was young, the men did not care for that. Oh, those were different times. In fact," Mrs.

Chesterton whispered as if it were a secret, "I do believe that's what set her against people—grown-up people in any case. She used to say, 'Children like me smart. Grown-ups want me stupid.' So, she never did marry, and she never did have many grown-up friends."

Mrs. Chesterton pushed a wisp of hair away from her forehead and placed it back over her head with a hairpin. Then she continued her story.

"Miss Tobias was rich to begin with, and since she never married, she not only kept her riches but gained more because she outlived her family. And what do you think she did with her money?" Mrs. Chesterton said softly.

"I don't know," I answered, my voice sounding loud.

"She bought books. Oh my, Miss Tobias loved reading. Read a book a day sometimes. But there was one kind of book she loved more than any other kind. Can you guess?"

45

Mrs. Chesterton about the summer reading list.

"When Miss McPhearson said such things to Miss Tobias about children's books, Miss Tobias would answer back, 'What kind of a teacher are you if you don't like children's books?' And Miss McPhearson would answer, 'I like useful books, not the nonsense you read.'

"But here comes the *real* unpleasantness. As I said, Miss Tobias had money. Miss McPhearson did not. They were family and so had obligations. Or so Miss Tobias would say. The Tobias family had a long tradition of leaving their money just to blood relations.

"One day at tea, Miss Tobias announced that she had made a new will, and that she had left Miss McPhearson all her treasure.

"Miss McPhearson—who was there—was *very* happy, though I myself wondered at that word 'treasure.' Later I said to Miss Tobias, 'I hope you are not going to tease

48

that young woman from your grave.' "

" 'Alice,' she said to me, 'she will find what she will find.' Then she laughed and would say no more.

"Well, then Miss Tobias died. And when the will was read, we learned that Miss Tobias had left Miss McPhearson five children's books."

Becky and I looked at each other. Five was exactly how many books had been stolen from the library. Then to be sure, I said, "Is that *all* she left?"

"All," said Mrs. Chesterton, "except for a note. I remember it well: 'Dear Niece: I have given into your care the best of children's books. They should lead you to the happiness you desire. But if not you, then for everyone. Children's books are full of promises.'

"Oh, my dears, Miss McPhearson wept! To be teased from the grave is cruel. She had expected so much more. But as it turned out, Miss Tobias had very little money.

8 ··· Mrs. Brattle's Confession

Becky and I were silent until we got out of the hotel. "Miss McPhearson got *five* books," Becky blurted out. "And five were stolen. Bet you anything she was the one who gave them to the library. She doesn't like kids' books and probably never thought they were worth much. You'll see, they were the same ones stolen. So that eliminates Miss Mc-Phearson. She wouldn't have to steal them back, would she? She could have just asked for them."

"And I still say Mrs. Brattle knows more than she's been telling," Becky grumbled. "I mean, maybe she stole the books and blamed me so no one would think of her. She takes them home with her, comes back the next morning, and calls the police and blames me. I think I once read a *Nancy Drew* story like that. I guess Mrs. Brattle could tell us a lot if she wanted to."

"Let's try her," I said, turning toward the library.

There were only a few people in the library. We even thought Mrs. Brattle wasn't there. But when we stood at her desk, by looking into the hall mirror we could see her in the children's room shelving books.

The children's room is smaller than the main room, but it has larger windows, and it's brighter. There are small tables and chairs, and pictures of Humpty-Dumpty, "Three Men in a Tub," and some Book Week posters on the wall. And there is a plaque that says: "A reader is not one who can read, but rather one who does read."

When we came up to her, I began, "Mrs. Brattle—"

She gave a jump. "Oh, it's you," she said,

volunteer. He thinks he knows books, but he doesn't. Then there's Mrs. Chesterton, who comes to clean at night. But the town doesn't really care about us. Oh, they brag about the library. But I'd be ashamed to tell you what I'm paid or what the book budget is.

"Now, I don't specialize in old books. That takes special training. Still, I know that sometimes valuable books are given to the sale, and they can be worth money. What I do is let someone who knows about such things look at them before every sale."

"Who's that?" Becky spoke up.

"Mr. Fitz-Williams. He's that nice man who runs the used book store in Allerton. Very honest and knows a lot about books.

"Usually, I make a list of my sale books and drop it in the mail to him. He tells me which ones are valuable. Once I had a book that was worth fifty dollars. He sells the expensive ones, takes a small fee, and gives the library the rest.

"This time I didn't have a spare moment to make out a list. A few days before the sale I just called and told him generally what I had, mentioning that a lot were from Miss Tobias."

Becky sensed the climax of the story. "What did he do?"

"Friday night—the night before the sale—after I put those last five books downstairs and went home, Mr. Fitz-Williams called me. All excited he was. Seems he thought that Miss Tobias had some very rare children's books in her collection. 'You might get thousands for those books,' he told me. Why, he wanted to come right out that night and look at them. But I said no, I was too tired. He said he'd stop by the first thing in the morning.

"I didn't know what to think. After considering, I called Mrs. Chesterton—she had been Miss Tobias's companion. I told her what Mr. Fitz-Williams had said—that the books might be worth a lot—and asked her if she knew anything about them. She said she didn't know, only that the old lady had given Miss McPhearson her best ones. I told her those were in the library too, but she didn't know anything about prices.

"Well, then I called Miss McPhearson just to be sure she wanted to give them to us," Mrs. Brattle went on.

"Did you tell her how valuable they might be?" I asked.

"Not exactly," admitted Mrs. Brattle. "I only said I might be able to get some money for them. She wanted to know how much. I said—and it was true—that I didn't know. She said, 'Sell them. Just please don't buy any more useless children's books with the money.' You see, she really didn't want them.

"So I just left them there. I suppose I shouldn't have. I never dreamed what would happen. After breakfast, I came here to check on things. Right away I saw that those five books were gone.

"It was my fault. I admit that. Then I made the further mistake of remembering that Becky had asked for *The Wizard of Oz*. I called the police.

"But after you left, Mr. Fitz-Williams did come. I told him what had happened. He was very upset. He was even more upset when he checked the remaining books. There was *nothing* worth his trouble. And when I described the missing books to him—he asked me lots of questions—he said they were worthless too."

"Worthless!" I cried. "Then how come someone took them?"

Mrs. Brattle shook her head. "I don't really know," she said. "I just don't. The world seems to be going crazy. Do you know this morning I heard that Ted Pegan's store, The Tree House, was broken into. Nothing missing. Just broken into. I can't explain anything anymore."

9 ... *The Secret of the Books*

That night, while the air was thick as chocolate pudding with the promise of rain, Becky and I had a meeting on the front porch.

Becky had gotten out a huge pad and a felt marker and was trying to put the whole thing together. She said that's the way real detectives did it.

First she wrote:

> 1. *Tobias gives books to Libr.*
> 2. *5 to Miss McPher.*

"That was just to tease her," I put in.

"That's what Mrs. Chesterton thought," said Becky. "Maybe Miss Tobias really meant it to be a big thing. Remember when you were four, you saved your used chewing gum and gave it to Mom for Christmas?"

That wasn't something I wanted to talk about.

Becky wrote some more:

3. *Miss McPher. hates books like that.*
4. *Gives them to Libr.*

"Point five," I said. "Mrs. Brattle tells Mr. Fitz-Williams about them."

"Six," said Becky. "He thinks they might be worth something."

"Seven. He tells Mrs. B. he wants to see them."

"But Mrs. Brattle can't be bothered."

Becky threw away the pad.

"But she must have gotten worried," I went on, "because she got up early to check the books. Five were gone."

"She blames me," said Becky.

"But the books turn out not to be worth anything anyway," I added.

61

There it was. It didn't make any sense at all.

"Maybe—" I tried, "maybe we're looking at things backwards. Miss Tobias is the one who said the books were valuable. Remember, she left a message with those books in her will about their bringing lots of happiness for people or something."

"Not bringing," Becky corrected. "*Leading* to happiness."

I thought for a while. Then something hit me. "Maybe *that's* it."

"What's it?" said Becky.

"Maybe those books aren't valuable—you know, to sell—but maybe they *lead* to something," I said. "I don't know what. The point is, maybe it's something *in* the books that leads—clues or something."

"They're all so different," said Becky.

"Did you ever read them?" I challenged her.

Becky considered, "You mean we should read them and see if they have any clues?" she asked.

62

"Come on, Becky. We might find something. I'll even read *Treasure Island* and *The Wind in the Willows*. I think they're the biggest."

She began to catch my mood. "Okay," she said. "I'll read *Winnie-the-Pooh*, *Through the Looking Glass*, and *The Wizard of Oz*. They shouldn't be hard to find."

Just then Gramp came out to the porch. "Anyone for checkers?" he offered. Checkers is his favorite game. But we weren't in any mood to think about games.

Getting hold of the books was easy. We actually had *Winnie-the-Pooh* (bottom of the closet), and some friends had *Treasure Island* and *The Wizard of Oz*. We got the rest from the library.

It wasn't exactly work reading those books. And they were a lot more fun than *Curious Facts About Ohio*. Becky started with *Winnie-the-Pooh*, while I began *Treasure Island*. But she kept interrupting me. "Listen to this," she'd say, cracking up and then reading something out loud.

I didn't care. I was reading about pirates, Long John Silver, Jim Hawkins, and the rest. But searching for treasure didn't leave much time for laughs, and I finally had to get away from Becky.

The fact is, I couldn't put *Treasure Island* down. But just as they were looking at the heaps of gold in Ben Gunn's cave, my dad made me go to bed. I finished the book with a flashlight under the covers. It's the best way to read anyway.

The next morning Becky began *Through the Looking Glass*. As she read it, she kept stopping and saying, "This is so crazy—crazy backwards," until *I* nearly went crazy backwards.

"Look," I finally told her. "You read your books on one side of the house, and I'll read mine on the other." She agreed, but every once in a while she'd shout out, "Crazy!"

Now I was reading *The Wind in the Willows*. It was like eating the best ice cream after the best pizza. It was a book about having friends—even though the best friends are animals.

I was still reading that when Becky started *The Wizard of Oz*. She didn't *say* much about it, but every once in a while she'd put the book down and stare. Finally, I had to ask what she was staring at.

"I keep wishing our street would turn to gold," she said.

It only took us two days to read all five books. Then, after getting some exercise out on the playing field, we got down to what we had to do. "Okay," I said. "What are they about?"

"*Winnie-the-Pooh*," she began, "is about some pretend animals who have adventures. Not real adventures, pretend adventures. There's a character named Eyore, a donkey who *wants* to worry about everything. And Piglet, a pig who gets nervous about everything. At first I thought it was going to be too young for me. But you know what? I know two Eyores and five Piglets myself.

It's really a great, funny book—like a long birthday party."

"Go on," I said.

"*Through the Looking Glass* is about this girl Alice who goes behind a mirror and finds herself in a place where everything is backwards. A place where you run fast just to stay still. Actually, it's all a chess game, and Alice is on the white side against the red— the Red Queen, that is. Alice wins."

"What about *The Wizard of Oz?*"

"That's about a girl too—Dorothy. She gets picked up by a storm and goes to the Land of Oz. She has all these great, magical adventures before she finds a way to get home. Even though it's magic, it seems very real, like it could happen to anyone. And it's much better than the movie."

Then it was my turn. "*Treasure Island* is all about pirate gold and how a boy—sort of like me—and a pirate chief, Long John Silver—he has a wooden leg—tries to steal treasure. It's really exciting."

"Did they get the treasure?"

"Sure. In Ben Gunn's cave. The boy is fantastically brave.

"*The Wind in the Willows* is hard to describe. It's about these animals, mostly Rat, Mole, and Mr. Toad. Toad has some hilarious adventures. Mole and Rat just feel good being alive. I don't know—it made *me* feel good."

And that was that. We were done.

"You thought the stories would have a clue in them," Becky reminded me.

"They all have talking animals," I said. "Except *Treasure Island*."

"They're all written by British authors," said Becky, "except *The Wizard of Oz*."

"They all have maps in the front of the books," I put in, leafing through the books all laid out in front of us. "Except *Through the Looking Glass*."

"They all have kids as important characters," said Becky. "Except *The Wind in the Willows*."

68

And finally I said, "They are one long story, except *Winnie-the-Pooh*."

We were getting nowhere. "What about treasure?" I tried. "It's in *Treasure Island*. What about the others?"

Becky considered. "In *The Wizard of Oz*, Dorothy was looking for a way to get home."

"That doesn't sound like a treasure to me," I said.

"In a way it is. She was looking for the silver slippers. Only they were on her feet all along. They really were treasures."

"That's two," I agreed. "In *The Wind in the Willows*, it's not exactly a treasure, but Mole and Rat get lost in the Wild Wood looking for this Mr. Badger's house. They only find it by tripping over Badger's foot scraper. They sure act like it's treasure."

"That's three!" sang out Becky, getting excited. "And in *Winnie-the-Pooh*, Eyore loses his tail. Everybody looks for it, and they find it in Owl's tree house."

"But there's no finding of treasure in

Through the Looking Glass," I said, frustrated. "It doesn't fit."

"Toby," said Becky hopefully, "maybe *Through the Looking Glass* was a mistake. It's so different from the others."

We thought about that for a while.

It's a funny thing. You can think and think about something, some idea, and nothing works until all of a sudden you see it differently. That's what happened. It came to me—just like that—and it was something Becky had said.

"It *was* a mistake," I said. "Because that's what it's about. Treasure. Miss Tobias's treasure. Someone is using those stories to try and find it too."

"How do you know?"

"Because," I said, "that crook already looked in the wrong place twice, that's why. And we should have guessed it before!"

10 ··· A Treasure Hunt

"Where did I say they found the pirate treasure in *Treasure Island?*" I asked Becky, trying to get her to figure it out the way I had.

"You said in Ben Gunn's cave."

As soon as she said that, I ran to the back of the house where we kept old newspapers and brought back the top bundle. Then I searched until I found Sunday's edition. Turning to the Checkertown page, I pointed to the headline that read:

ROBBERIES

"You see," I pointed out, "it wasn't *one* robbery. It was *two*. Read the story. Not

about the library—the other one." And Becky read: *"Mike Weikof, owner of the Gun Shop, reported a break-in at his gun and sporting goods store Friday evening. When he arrived at his store the next morning, he found the lock had been forced and someone had entered. Nothing, however, had been taken."*

"It makes no sense," said Becky, puzzled.

"Becky," I said, "the Treasure was in Ben

72

Gunn's cave. Get it. Ben *Gunn*. Gun Shop."

"But they said nothing was taken," cried Becky. "It's just a coincidence."

"Remember *Winnie-the-Pooh?*" I said. "What was that treasure? You said they were looking for something."

"Eyore's tail."

"Where did they find it?"

"Owl's tree house."

"Becky," I said, trying to keep calm, "remember when we were talking to Mrs. Brattle? She said something about how Ted Pegan's tree service place was broken into. What does he call the store? Mrs. Brattle said it."

Becky thought for a moment. "The Tree House," she said. "And nothing was taken from there either."

"You see," I said, *"that's* what it's all about. I bet you anything that Miss Tobias hid a treasure somewhere in town. And you know, the way you find treasure is by using maps. It's the *maps* in the books that can tell us where it's hidden. Maybe it's the rest of her money!"

"You mean," said Becky, "someone's going to look for a foot scraper like in *The Wind in the Willows?*"

"It's not the *what*," I said. "It's the *where*. And that's why you have to use the maps."

Becky considered the whole thing. *"Through the Looking Glass* doesn't have a map," she insisted.

"Don't worry about that one," I told her. "Everything else fits. In fact, it makes it easier. Only one of the books probably works, and that isn't it."

For the rest of the day and into the night we studied the maps in the four books, but Becky kept raising objections.

"I think it's a great idea," she said, "except for one thing. If I had a map of England, I couldn't find much of anything in Mexico, could I?"

I had to agree.

"Toby, look at these maps. They're all

74

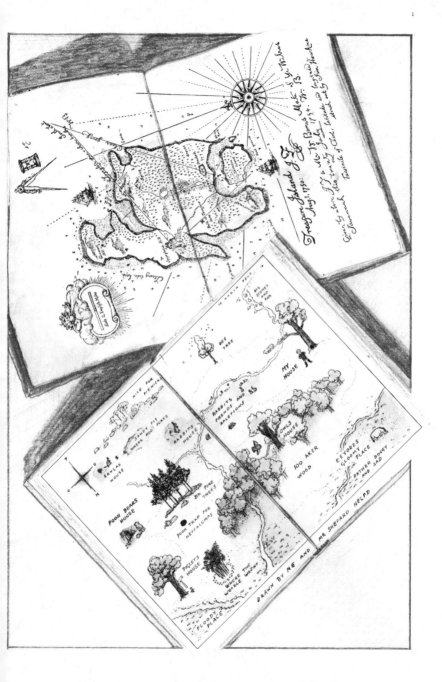

from different places. They aren't even real. How can you find a real place with pretend maps?"

"They're clues," I insisted. "All we have to do is figure them out. And we have to do it before the thief does."

11 ··· More Clues

"Okay," Becky challenged me, pushing the map of Oz over. "You do it. Where are the silver slippers?"

I studied the map carefully. "Where did Dorothy find them?"

"Over here," said Becky, putting her finger on the place where Dorothy landed on the Wicked Witch of the East. "She put the shoes on there, but she didn't discover their magic till later. She wears them all through the book."

"You see," I said, "all we have to do is find the witch's house and we've solved the mystery. Any witches in town?"

"That's dumb, and you know it," said

Becky. "What about an emerald city. A greenhouse!" she suddenly cried. "What about that?"

"I don't think that's right. Where did she learn about the slippers' magic?"

"In the palace of Glinda the Good."

"Come on, Becky, *think*," I shouted. "Where would you look for silver slippers?"

"There are no such things," she shot back.

"A jewelry store," I yelled at her. "Miss Tobias was rich. She could go into a jewelry store anytime she wanted."

"It won't work, Toby," said Becky. "Even if you're right, the thief might be looking for *The Wind in the Willows* treasure while we're waiting for the person to go after the *Oz* treasure."

I wasn't going to give up. "I still say it's a jewelry store. Now, all we have to do is find where the thing from *The Wind in the Willows* is." I went back to the map.

"You said it was in the Wild Wood. There are no woods around here."

"Becky," I pleaded, "remember that sign in the library? 'A reader is not one who can read, but rather one who does read.' We have to *read* the clues. It's the *only* way."

She made herself think. "Well, maybe there's a Mr. Badger in town," she suggested. She went to get the phone book. Sure enough, there was a J. Badger on Fourth Street.

"Maybe you're right," she admitted.

"See," I said, "now we know the next two places. Don't you see, Becky? Mrs. Chesterton said that everybody thought Miss Tobias was rich. But when she died, she didn't have much at all. Even Gramp said that. I bet she hid it all somewhere. That's what happened. Mrs. Chesterton said Miss Tobias was only teasing Miss McPhearson. So she left the books as a puzzle. Remember that will? 'May they *lead* to happiness.' That's exactly what one of the books can do."

"Which one?" said Becky.

I ignored her. "But Miss McPhearson doesn't see it. She hates kids' books. She

80

gives them away. I'll bet you anything that's what Miss Tobias *wanted* to happen. Maybe she even planned it that way. But you see, *somebody* else figured it out. And that person stole the books."

"I still think you're missing something," Becky said.

"And you're just saying that because *I* figured it out," I told her. I was so mad that I went inside and grabbed the day's paper. I turned to the Checkertown section—and I almost died. Because, sure enough, there was a new headline:

MORE ROBBERIES

Another in the continuing series of mysterious break-ins took place in Checkertown in recent days. On Tuesday night Noble's Lumber Company reported that its main office had been entered. Nothing, however, appeared to be missing. The next night police reported that Miss Ranck's Royal Shoe Store was entered, though once more nothing was taken. Police admit that they have no clues and are greatly puzzled by this rash of odd crimes.

"Lumber company," said Becky, when I showed her the article. "What's that got to do with anything?"

"Mole found Badger in the Wild Wood," I reminded her. "Get it—lumber—wood."

Becky actually let out a moan. "And it wasn't a jewelry store for the silver slippers. It was a shoe store!"

12 ··· *The Biggest Clue*

We felt cheated. We didn't know who the thief was, or even what the treasure was. And when Becky reminded me that we still didn't know how *Through the Looking Glass* fit in, it began to look as if we might be wrong about everything. I mean, I started to think the puzzle *had* to work on all of them if it meant anything. But it didn't.

Still, we had a feeling that the thief didn't know any more than we did. After all, the newspaper kept reporting that nothing was taken. It looked as if Miss Tobias had tricked everyone. Nobody could untangle her puzzle.

We talked about it over and over again. Oh, we did other things. We had fun, played, and saw friends. But the question was always in the back of our minds, "Who stole *The Wizard of Oz?*"

Then, to make things worse, it began to rain. After so many hot days, this should have been a relief. The trouble was that it rained not for one day but for three. There was nothing to do.

On the third rainy day, Becky and I were sitting on the porch doing nothing more interesting than watching the water drip. Things were that dull. Finally, I said, "How about a game of something?"

"What?" she asked.

I tried to think of a game we hadn't played recently. "Stratego?" She shook her head. "Sorry?" Again, no. "Checkers?"

"I don't care," she said. "Anything."

I brought out the checker set and put out the pieces. Then I held up my fists. She touched the hand with the black pieces.

"You first," I said, waiting for her to move. But I could see she really didn't want to play.

"Come on," I called, trying to get her going. "Make it a battle. We're two armies." I waved my hand over the board. "It's a *real* battle. Don't think of it as a board. It's a map."

She nodded.

Then, out of nowhere, she screamed—*"That's it!"* I was so startled that I knocked over the board.

"What are you talking about?" I scolded.

Becky was leaping up and down as if she were skipping rope. "You were right," she kept saying. "You were right!" And grabbing the checkerboard, she held it over her head. "It *is* a map," she yelled. "They *all* have maps!"

I still didn't know what she was talking about.

"Don't you see?" she cried. "All the books had maps except one of them. That's what I kept saying. But the chessboard *is* a map. So, *Through the Looking Glass* has a map, too. All the maps were of *other* places. But this map is right here—Checkertown. Toby, isn't a

85

chessboard the same as a checkerboard?"

"I guess so," I admitted.

"Remember what you read me from *Curious Facts About Ohio?*" she prodded. "How Checkertown was laid out just like a checkerboard?"

86

Becky fetched *Through the Looking Glass* and returned with the book open to the chess problem.

"All the other books had people finding things," I reminded her. "You didn't say anybody found anything in this one."

Instead of answering, Becky turned to the title page. *"Through the Looking Glass,"* it read. Then, in smaller letters—but still part of the title—it said: *And What Alice Found There.*

"That's what she found," insisted Becky. "The *whole* story. The story is that she wins. And it tells *where* she wins right on the chess map." She handed me the book. "In the story," she added, "Alice beats the Red Queen."

"Hey!" I said. "Miss McPhearson has red hair!"

"And look here," I added, *reading* the chess problem in the book. "It tells just where the pieces moved. I mean, the end of the story is the last move. It takes place right here," I said, pointing to one of the squares on the map.

"What's that spot on the Checkertown map?" asked Becky.

I went and got the phone book with the town map in it. Then we set the chess map (from the book) and the town map (from the phone book) side by side so the squares matched. We looked at one, then the other.

"The last move is where Alice beats the Red Queen," said Becky, and she put her finger down on the Checkertown map.

"That's where the library is," I said.

For a moment we just thought about it.

"All we have to do is figure out *where* in the library the treasure is hidden," Becky said softly.

Even as she said that, I knew. I really did. "That big mirror between the library main room and the children's room, remember? I bet the treasure is right behind the mirror. I mean, a mirror is a looking glass, isn't it?"

"*Through the Looking Glass,*" Becky giggled.

"*And What Alice Found There,*" I added.

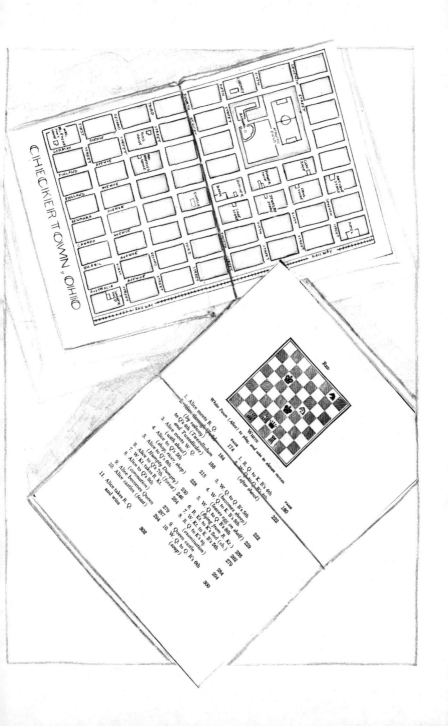

13 ··· *Through the Looking Glass*

"Let's get it!" cried Becky, ready to go right then.

But I had a different idea. "I bet the thief hasn't figured it out yet," I said.

"Well, let's go before he does," said Becky. "Come *on!*"

"Becky," I said. "We have to use the treasure as bait." She looked at me queerly, until I added, "Aren't we trying to find out *who* took the books in the first place?"

"I suppose so."

"The honor of your name?"

"Toby, I don't care anymore."

"Yes you do. Just sit down and listen." She did reluctantly, but I knew I'd have to talk fast, or she'd be off and running. "You know the part in the paper that has Checkertown news? Well, maybe we could call the woman who writes it and tell her about that thing I read in the book—about Checkertown and the checkerboard. If they printed it, and if the thief read it, he might get the same idea we got. It would be a trap."

"Too many *ifs*," Becky warned.

"We could still try," I said. "Mom knows the woman who writes that page. We could call her."

Becky still wasn't very enthusiastic. But the way I figured it, it was the best chance we had.

Anyway, I got the reporter's name from the paper, found her phone number, and called. "This is Toby Almano," I said. "You know my mother." Then I told her that I had been reading a book about Ohio and that there was something in it about Checkertown. "I just thought you might like it for your newspaper column," I suggested. I held my breath until she said, "Why don't you read it to me?"

I had the book right there, of course, so I read the paragraph to her. She thought it was really interesting.

"Do you think you might print it?" I asked.

"I might," she said. "People always like that sort of thing." And she asked me to read it all over again so she could write it down.

"Will she print it?" asked Becky when I hung up.

"Maybe," was all I could say.

Right off, we tore over to the library. We didn't care that it was still raining. When we got there, Mrs. Brattle was at her desk. She gave us a nod, but didn't seem to pay us any further mind.

We headed for the children's room. As we walked down the little hallway past the mirror, we had no doubts. We just knew. The mirror was tall and skinny, with a decorated, heavy frame full of fancy spiral designs. It *had* to be right.

I looked back over my shoulder at Mrs. Brattle. She was watching us. I nudged Becky back into the children's room.

"I think she suspects something," Becky whispered, and she snuck out into the hall—only to have Mrs. Brattle look up again. Becky came back fast. "We'll have to do *something*," she said. "Go ask her a question," she told me. "While she's busy with you, I'll look behind the mirror."

Becky hung around the mirror while I went over to Mrs. Brattle. When the librarian looked up, I said, "I'm trying to find something about—dinosaurs in the encylopedia. Can you help me? I can't find anything."

"Are you sure you spelled it correctly?" she asked.

I had to think for a second to make sure I got it *wrong:* "D I N A S A U R," I said.

She frowned, then spelled it correctly: "D I N O S A U R. Try that," she said, and went back to her work.

Not having much choice, I went to the

encylopedia that was behind her desk and started going through it. "I still can't find it," I said.

Mrs. Brattle got up from her desk and started to help me. As soon as she turned her back, I saw Becky trying to look behind the mirror. I was dying to watch—I expected a crash any second—but I had to continue the act I had started. As it was, Mrs. Brattle found the section very fast.

"Thanks!" I said, almost yelling as I caught sight of Becky diving back into the children's room.

I spent a few seconds pretending to read the article, then strolled out to the lobby. Becky joined me there.

"Well?" was all I said.

She just grinned.

"What is it?"

"I'm not sure," she said. "But whatever it is, it's stuck behind the mirror alright. It's about halfway up and wrapped in green."

14 ··· Setting the Trap

The Allerton newspaper reaches town at about three o'clock. The day after we had called the reporter, Becky and I were waiting for it at one o'clock. When it finally came, we bought the first copy, ripped it open to the Checkertown page, and there it was—right in the middle of the column:

An old book about Ohio reminds us of how Checkertown got its name: "The railroad section manager, who planned the town and laid out its streets, was so taken with the game of checkers that he designed the town streets in checkerboard fashion. Eight streets running one way and eight the other."

96

Like a shot, we tore down to the library, through the hall, past the mirror, and into the children's room. Becky even managed a squint behind the mirror. Whatever *it* was, it hadn't moved.

Becky and I sat down at a table that was in a perfect place. If anyone fooled with the mirror we would see right away. But two hours went by and nothing happened.

Then at five o'clock, Mrs. Brattle came into the room and told us the library was closing for suppertime. We had to go out with her.

She locked the doors behind us, said, "Good night," and walked off.

Becky pinched my arm.

"What's that for?" I said, jumping.

She pointed at Mrs. Brattle. "She's got the newspaper with her!"

So of course we didn't dare leave. Instead, we sat down on the front steps and waited. Then, maybe ten minutes later, Becky jumped up as if she'd been stung. "There's a back door," she cried, and took off. "I'll watch that."

An hour passed and still nobody came. But to be sure, we had to stay—one of us at either side of the building. Every once in a while we'd check on each other.

At a quarter to seven Mr. Neal appeared. He nodded to me as he went up the front steps. He was also carrying the newspaper.

"Where's Mrs. Brattle?" I blurted out.

"She's not feeling very well," he said. "She asked me to work tonight."

I tried to follow him inside, but he wouldn't let me. "The library's closed until seven," he said firmly.

I ran out back to tell Becky.

"She's not sick," Becky insisted. "You'll see. She'll come. It's just another alibi."

As soon as Mr. Neal opened up we ran inside. We headed straight for the children's room, stopping first for a quick squint behind the mirror. *It* was still there.

We got some books and pretended to be

98

reading. There wasn't much else we could do. A few times Mr. Neal came in to give us dirty looks, but he didn't say anything. That is, not until a few minutes to nine. Then he came in to announce, "We're closing. Did you want to check something out?"

We got up slowly and went to the door. I kept watching Becky, hoping she'd think of something. But she didn't. As it was, Mr. Neal just about pushed us out and locked the door.

"Now what?" I said.

"The back door," said Becky. And off she went to the back of the library. I followed. But when we got there, the door was locked.

"Don't worry," said Becky. Going to the door, she put her hand to the knob, jiggled it, and to my surprise it opened.

"Where'd you learn that?" I asked.

"Don't look at me like that," she said. "A lot of kids know how to do it. I can have *some* secrets, can't I?"

"Becky—" I warned.

"We can't give up now," she whispered, pulling me inside and shutting the door behind us.

We were in the basement section where the book sale had been. There were even a few books left from the sale—they looked sort of like the remains of a big meal. Everything was quiet.

We stood there while our eyes got used to the dark. From up above we could hear someone walking. We figured it was Mr. Neal. Then we heard the front door slam. We were alone alright—right where we weren't supposed to be.

"Let's go," whispered Becky. She reached out and took my hand. Finding the steps, she led the way up. Though we tried to be quiet, we kept making all kinds of noises. All the same, in a few seconds we were standing in the main room.

After the last few days of rain, the skies were so clear that there was a lot of moonlight. It made everything in the room soft and golden. It reminded me of what Miss Tobias used to say, "The moon is the best listener."

Still holding hands, Becky and I made our way to the children's room, getting there with only one small smash against a table.

We sat down, leaned back against some shelves, and faced the mirror.

Neither of us said anything.

As we waited, the moonlight began to shift until it seemed to be shining directly on the mirror in the hallway—as if it were pointing to that special green package.

We could see everything. Anyone who came even close to the mirror would be spotted right away.

"Now what?" I said. My stomach gurgled from hunger.

"Shhh!" said Becky.

Figuring someone just had to come, we sat back, waited, and listened.

15 ⋯ The Thief Takes the Bait

I think we were both glad to have the moonlight and that the two of us were together.

"You scared?" I whispered to Becky.

"Not really," she said.

"You're lying," I told her.

"A little."

"As much as me?" I said.

She giggled. "I guess so."

"What do we do if somebody *does* come?"

"Turn on the lights," said Becky. "The switch is by the door."

"What if nobody comes?"

"Somebody will."

"Then what?"

She didn't answer *that* question.

"Who do you think it will be?" I asked her.

"Mrs. Brattle," she said right off.

"Boy," I said, "when you don't like someone, you don't change your mind."

We waited some more. I thought about the librarian, and I admit I felt Becky was right. Mrs. Brattle was always saying she didn't get paid enough. And she did have too much to do alone. She had expected to get something from Miss Tobias, too. She must have thought those five books were worth something. Then she figured out the map part.

"How long are we going to stay here?" I said to Becky.

"As long as we have to."

"We're in for some big trouble if we're caught here."

She didn't say anything.

"You know," I said, "if you're right about Mrs. Brattle, I'll feel sorry for her. She could use the money."

"She's a thief," said Becky.

"Nobody's stolen anything that's worth anything yet," I reminded her.

"That's not the—" Becky didn't finish her sentence. There had been a sound. Then another.

There wasn't much doubt about it. Someone was coming into the building, right through the front door. We pushed ourselves down against the floor.

The hall lights burst on. And a second later, Mrs. Brattle appeared. She walked halfway across the main room, then stopped. I was sure she looked into the children's room. But she moved on. We couldn't tell where she was, but we could hear papers rattling.

A few seconds later Mrs. Brattle walked back across the room. The lights snapped off. The front door slammed shut.

Only then did I realize that Becky was squeezing my hand so hard it hurt.

"Did she go to the mirror?" she managed to say.

"Not that I saw."

"She must have known we were here."

"She couldn't have."

"It's a trick," said Becky angrily. "That's all it is!"

"I don't know," I said. "I just want to get out of here." I stood up.

"Get down!" cried Becky, pulling at me. "It's a trick. She knows we're here. She wants us to go so she can come back and get the treasure."

"That's crazy," I objected. "She just came in here to get some work."

"You'll see," Becky insisted.

We argued back and forth, whispering furiously—until Becky grabbed my hand again. "Shhhh!"

I stopped to listen. "Now what?"

"I thought I heard something."

I listened, and sure enough, there *was* a squeak.

"The basement steps," Becky whispered. "The way we came in."

We had been scared when Mrs. Brattle had come. Well, we were scared again. For sure enough, with slow, careful steps, someone was coming out of the basement. This time no lights went on. All the same, whoever it was was coming into the main room.

Although we strained, we couldn't make out who it was. But one thing was certain. *Someone* was standing there. They even took a few steps toward the children's room.

Then a flashlight, pointing down to the floor, was turned on. Its beam of light moved around like a long pointy finger, coming to rest on the mirror. It seemed to poke about the mirror, and then it went out.

Whoever it was walked toward the mirror. Once again the flashlight went on, now jabbing at the mirror's frame. The person was looking behind the mirror. We saw a white hand flutter up, reach forward, give a jerk, and pull something out.

Where had I seen a hand like that before?

107

"Now!" screamed Becky.

We jumped up and raced toward the door. Becky flipped on the switch. Lights seemed to explode.

There stood the thief.

16 ... Who Stole
THE WIZARD OF OZ
and Why

It was hard to say who was more surprised, Mrs. Chesterton or us. We all just stood there, looking at each other. Mrs. Chesterton was the first to speak.

"What are you children doing here?" she asked, her voice soft and pleasant. "The library has been closed for some time now."

"What are *you* doing here?" Becky retorted.

"It's my job to be here," said Mrs. Chesterton. "I do the cleaning. I suppose I really should call the police—or Mrs. Brattle." She was holding one hand behind her back.

"If you do," I warned her, "you'll have to show them what you've taken."

"We put that note in the newspaper about the checkerboard map and Checkertown," said Becky.

Mrs. Chesterton looked at us. After a while, she said, "I didn't think of that. I would have, after a time. There's only one of me to think of things." She shook her head. She seemed even smaller than she was.

"Are you going to leave it?" asked Becky.

Mrs. Chesterton sighed. "I thought you were such nice children when you came to visit. What business is it of yours?"

"They blamed me for taking those five books," said Becky.

"I didn't know," said Mrs. Chesterton. "I am truly sorry. Believe me." She looked at us. "What do you children intend to do?"

Becky and I looked at each other. We really didn't know. But then I said, "If you leave it, we don't have to do anything."

"Or tell anybody," Becky added.

For the first time, Mrs. Chesterton brought her hand out from behind her back. She was holding the small package wrapped

110

in beautiful green paper. "You don't even know what it is, do you?" she said. "You haven't guessed *that*."

"No, we haven't," I said.

"I did," she said. "It's a treasure. A *true* treasure."

"It belongs to Miss McPhearson," said Becky.

"I thought you didn't like her," said Mrs. Chesterton. It was the only time she seemed angry. "She wouldn't care for it at all. In Miss Tobias's will it said: 'If not you, then for everyone.'"

"Are *you* everyone?" asked Becky.

Sadly, Mrs. Chesterton shook her head. "Miss McPhearson will only sell it. And become rich. And they will put it in a box, and nobody will be able to look at it. I would read it over and over again and love it. Treasures belong to people who treasure things."

I was beginning to feel all mixed up, as if *I* were the thief, taking the book from its rightful owner.

But carefully, Mrs. Chesterton placed the small package on a table.

"Why don't you open it," she said. "Don't you wish to see what it is?"

I looked at the green package. Then I went forward and carefully opened it. It was a book. A red book only a little bigger than a paperback. On the cover were some gold lines that ran all around its edge. In the middle of the front cover were three circles, one inside the other. In the very center of the inside circle was a picture of a girl holding a pig. It was just the same on the back cover, except in the middle circle was the picture of a cat—a cat smiling in the strangest way. Along the back edge of the book was printed the title: *Alice In Wonderland*.

"Isn't your name Alice?" asked Becky.

Mrs. Chesterton's eyes never left the book. Slowly, softly, she began to speak. "I was here in the library that Friday night cleaning. Mrs. Brattle called me and told me that Miss Tobias's five special books were

112

here. I took them back to my room. I knew right away that those books weren't worth anything. I knew it was a puzzle. Miss Tobias just wanted to tease. And I meant no harm—Miss McPhearson didn't want the books. I didn't even think anyone would notice they were gone. What I did know was that Miss Tobias had done something with her money. She bought that book. Not that she told me what she'd done. You see, I *was* Alice against the Red Queen. But the other Alice won—and for me it's not to be so," she said.

Carefully, without looking back, Mrs. Chesterton went down the steps, leaving the book with us.

17 ··· How the Story Ends

I didn't know what to do. I felt awful.
And I didn't have to guess that Becky felt the
same. Mrs. Chesterton loved the book. But
she couldn't have it. Miss McPhearson probably hated it. But it was meant for her.

Or was it? "Becky," I said. "Maybe Miss
Tobias *wanted* to trick Miss McPhearson into
giving away those books. You know, giving
the treasure to her so she wouldn't want it."

"She did say," agreed Becky, 'if not you,
then for everyone.'"

We looked at the book the way Mrs.
Chesterton had left it, with the cat smiling
up so weirdly.

"Let's just leave it," Becky whispered.

She got a pen and paper from Mrs. Brattle's desk and wrote: "For everyone in Checkertown." And then she said, "If they want to, *they* can figure it out."

Two days later there was an article in the Allerton paper. It wasn't in the back part, though. It was front-page news. The headline read:

MYSTERIOUS DISCOVERY

Very Rare Book Found

Mrs. R.B. Brattle, Checkertown librarian, announced the discovery of Lewis Carroll's ALICE IN WONDERLAND *in the library. Very few copies exist. Mr. John Fitz-Williams, rare book dealer, has appraised the book as being worth $15,000. As to how the Checkertown library came to this treasure, Mrs. Brattle was quite frank. "We don't know," she said. "It just appeared mysteriously. But we do hope everyone will enjoy it."*

"Do you kids know anything about this?" asked Gramp when he read the story. It was clear that he suspected something.

Becky looked at me. I looked at Becky. But we didn't say a thing. And he never asked again.

But what about Miss McPhearson? What happened to her? That summer she quit teaching and went off somewhere to work with computers. So Becky never was in her class. And Mrs. Chesterton? We've seen her in the library many times, looking at *that* book.

We've read it too. And it *is* a treasure.

It's like Miss Tobias used to say, "A good children's book is a book of promises."

And promises are to keep . . . and share.

Avi, a librarian at Trenton State College, is also a teacher of children's literature and often performs readings of his books in schools and libraries. He has written many books for young people, including EMILY UPHAM'S REVENGE, and NO MORE MAGIC, both of which won Mystery Writers of America Special Awards, and MAN FROM THE SKY, another Knopf Capers book.

Avi lives in New Hope, Pennsylvania. He is the father of two teenage sons.

Other Capers books by Knopf:

———————

Man from the Sky, AVI
Mystery of the Plumed Serpent, BARBARA BRENNER
Invasion of the Brain Sharpeners, PHILIP CURTIS
Invasion from Below the Earth, PHILIP CURTIS
Rosie's Double Dare, ROBIE H. HARRIS
The Mystery on Bleeker Street, WILLIAM H. HOOKS
The Case of the Weird Street Firebug, CAROL RUSSELL LAW
Running Out of Time, ELIZABETH LEVY
Running Out of Magic with Houdini, ELIZABETH LEVY
The Secret Life of the Underwear Champ, BETTY MILES
The Robot and Rebecca:
The Mystery of the Code-Carrying Kids, JANE YOLEN
The Robot and Rebecca and the Missing Owser, JANE YOLEN
The Boy Who Spoke Chimp, JANE YOLEN

———————

"I hope the Capers signal a return to the
important role light, easy-to-read fiction has in
getting children into the reading habit."

DONALD J. BISSETT,
Children's Literature Center,
Wayne State University